Someone New

The Gifted, Volume 1

Londa Cele

Published by LondaCeleNovels, 2023.

SOMEONE NEW

First edition. March 9, 2023.

Copyright © 2023 Londa Cele.

ISBN: 979-8215051740

Written by Londa Cele.

Table of Contents

Somebody New

Sifiso and Amanda were together for 8 years before they ended. In doing so, Sifiso moved back home to KZN, finding a new job and tucking the ring he was going to use to propose to Amanda in his pocket. But as soon as he hit his hometown he was fortunate enough to be hosted by his parents since his return, but now, it was time to move out before they rubbed each other the wrong way and things became sour. Sifiso found his own place and began to spread his wings of independence for a second time. What could one say other than that they were proud of their Sifiso and his achievements, even more so now that he'd done them so close to home.

•••

"**S**o, what seems to be the problem?"

"I still can't get over her, despite how far I've moved on with my life," Sfiso sighed.

"Is that so, and why do you think that could be?" his therapist asked.

"I honestly do not have any idea, if I did, I don't think I'd find myself in this situation"

He chewed his pen and listened.

"It's also this stupid ring?"

"Ring?"

"Yes, ring?" Sifiso clarified. "I was going to propose before I found myself in a new province when reality set in and showed us that our relationship can't work. I know what you're about to ask, but if we can't even make things work out together in the presence of each other, what were the odds of us making it work long-distance?"

The therapist shrugged. "So you two still keep in contact?"

"If it so happens, but none of us will go out of our way to talk to each other, that's for sure. Well, that I can only assume is the case because that's how things feel like."

"Hmm, I see,"

"I don't pay you to see, I'd just like to put that out there"

"Here's what you need to keep in mind, the two of you may not be together, in fact, maybe trying two different methodologies of moving on, but that doesn't mean that your life is stagnant just because she's not in it. As for the ring? Get rid of it, the longer you keep it, the more you hold on to something that's no longer there, causing nobody but yourself some pain and hurt."

And that's what Sifiso did. And in doing so, a whole new world opened up for him, mainly his world with his newfound love, Pinky. She was beautiful. She was smart; she was out of his league, in fact, most of all, she made him spend most of the day questioning the simple yet complicated emotion known to most

2

as love. Few people were as loving and supportive, if possible, as Pinkster. She was a diamond, one that had found him and not the other way around. But it should have been that way because right now, ever since Sifiso had moved back home, since being retrenched and starting afresh in the coastal city, where the sea washed all his bad luck and sin away for him to start over. Pinky remained a breadwinner, despite being tasked with the duty to feed her sister's kids. She kept it together and helped out at home. Gave her sister money when she needed it and "look after her man" all thanks to the hours she put in between 8 and 5 on Monday to Friday at the Garbage Company or to put it more respectfully since she made all the money at a Refuse Centre.

"You really don't have to take me to therapy, I insist... sit down"

"It's not like I've got anything better to do, I insist. After all, how else am I going to get the real you?" she giggled, scrapping her car keys and purse off the kitchen table simultaneously.

"This is not going to end well," Sfiso mumbled.

"What was that?" Pinky asked, locking the gate.

"I asked if you are sure you have everything?"

Pinky nodded before they headed for the lift at the end of the hall. Although there was nothing wrong being done by Pinky, if anything, she was just being a supportive partner most people wished they could trade their own for her forward-thinking. And Sfiso had said nothing about his partner that should warrant him to be afraid to bring her along. The biggest problem he had, if he had any, was the subject Dr Woods was incapable of letting go. The minute he'd entered, they'd start talking about Amanda and his inability to get over her. Who knew one visit to the doctor could make for such a quiet ride home? At least he'd listened to what he'd been told and gotten rid of the bling, as hard as it was, it might've been the only action to save his relationship, he thought to himself as they drove back home. "Can you stop here? I want to get us something to eat because I can bet my life savings that there's no way you're cooking in this mood," he said, pointing at a pizza joint. After deciding on what they'd eat, they parted ways. Pinky was stuck in the car as she waited for the drive-thru to move while Sfiso took his chances on foot entering the establishment. A few minutes passed before Sfiso's thoughts were interrupted by a tap on his shoulder.

"Hey Brenda, what are the odds of seeing you here?"

"I'd give you the numbers, but I'm too hungry to do the math," she told him, returning the hug.

The two friends rendered themselves noisy even though there was no need to as they caught up, making it more of an uncomfortable experience than it already was for hungry people waiting to buy pizza.

"What are you doing here anyway, aren't you meant to be in Jo'burg?"

"I'm on leave. I'm down here to help with a wedding,"

"Yeah well, I'm not surprised you were always the one that enjoyed going out and stuff in varsity so it makes sense," Sfiso shrugged.

"Oh, speaking about going out and stuff, how often do you go out or do you still lock yourself indoors, and this time I'm sure past the time with porn and masturbation?"

"I go out a lot, mind you, so no. No masturbation for me," Sfiso said confidently.

"Is it?" Brenda nodded as they joined the line to wait for their pizza just after ordering.

"I'm not sure if I should even do this, but either way, I get in shit if I do and I get in shit if I don't. How is it that my two best friends fucked up eight years together?" Brenda sighed.

"B, what are you on about? You're talking to yourself and scaring me," Sfiso said, moving back.

Brenda stared at him silently, and he stared back in confusion. "I doubt you've received it yet, but even if you have and have been ignoring it, at least there's now proof that you got it,"

"Got what?" Pinky asked, snatching the envelope out of Sfiso's hands. "I decided to come join you here, Drive-thru is going nowhere."

"Pinky, meet Brenda, a friend of mine from varsity who'd let me copy a few notes here and there,"

"A few?"

"Brenda, meet Pinky, my partner," Sfiso said, waving his arms to the people in question.

"Nice to meet you, and thank you for saving his right arm," she smiled.

"F'tsek,"

"Don't mention it," Pinky said, rolling her eyes. "So what does this serve as proof of, want us to open it?" she smiled at Sfiso.

"It's his invite to Amanda's wedding," Brenda finally spoke, putting an end to the awkward silence before leaving to go fetch her food as her number was called up. "It was nice to see you again, hope it won't be the last," she finished, passing by her friend for what hopefully wouldn't be the last time.

"And then?" Pinky asked.

"Can we talk about this some other time, we still need to drive home and I wanna eat my food while it's still warm,"

"No problem," she said, snatching the boxes from him. "We'll eat right here, problem solved. Besides, I'm going to need to sit down to hear your explanation for this?" she said waving the envelope in his face.

2

Sfiso sat down, in any other situation this would've been a cringe-worthy moment but as he sunk into the leather of Dr Woods's furniture there was nothing else he could do, chose to do, except wait to be given the attention he needed to let loose.

"What seems to be the problem?" Dr Woods asked once he'd made himself comfortable.

The phrase was his default setting, almost like an ATM asking you to enter your pin whenever you wanted to withdraw money. There was so much to say, but it all fell into plan as soon as Woods began chewing on his pen.

"Brenda,"

"I don't think I follow, I'm going to need a little more context,"

"She's a mutual friend of Amanda and I and the reason things have turned south between Pinky and me,"

"Well, that sucks doesn't it,"

"The thing is, we met up by chance and caught up as good old friends do and then she took it as a great chance to invite me to Amanda's wedding,"

"Amanda's getting married?" Dr Woods asked in shock.

"That was my initial reaction as well, however, Pinky didn't share the same reaction and now thinks that I'm still in love with Amanda, which isn't the case,"

"And how do we know that?" Woods shrugged. "To be honest, I don't blame her, I'd also feel the same way if my ex's best friend popped out of nowhere to invite me to her friend's wedding out of the blue. Clearly, it would mean something is still going on, no?"

"No!"

"If you say so," Woods shrugged. "And how would you feel or better still do if the roles were reversed?"

"It's not going to happen. The fuck would Pinky be fraternising with her ex and 'friends' linking her to that past life. They broke up didn't they... he's in the past if he's getting married then it means that he's moving on. She should do the same or better still, he should learn to do the same without her,"

"I see," Woods bit his pen.

"She knew that coming into my life. As the saying goes, new man, new life,"

"And Brenda?"

"No, Brenda is different, Brenda is a friend, always has and always will be. In fact, she's more like a sister and if there is anything to take away from this, it's how this should be used as a teaching moment to stop Pinky from being jealous of all the other women in my life and understand that she's the only one that matters. If she can't curb her jealousy or we can't work around or with it, then it spells doom for our relationship,"

"How so?"

"What do you mean, how so? Because there's no one else but Pinky, if she's going to feel threatened by anything that menstruates once a month then she's not ready to be in a relationship with me at the least because she's going to keep comparing herself to Amanda even when there is no need to because what attracted me to her and what attracted me to Amanda were two completely different things"

"Are we sure it's her and not you doing the comparing?"

"What do you mean?"

"You were about to tell me what the reasons that attracted you to both women are?" Woods cleared his throat, adjusting his seating.

The silence in the room was thick and stuffy, but it didn't seem to bother the doctor who seemed somewhat accustomed to it as he waited for a response from Sfiso.

"You're doing that thing of yours where you twist my words again?"

"Not at all," Woods said, waving his arms. "But if you're not ready, we can address it another time. We can still focus on your thoughts and feelings regarding the wedding,"

"Pinky is amazing..."

"But?"

"What do you mean, but?"

"You wouldn't see me so urgently if she was simply amazing. Your friend gifting you an invitation to your exes if we can call her that, the news of the wedding was unfortunate but not the end of the world and something that could've easily been resolved without my involvement. So what seems to be the catch?"

"I'm scared if I tell you, you'll judge me,"

"I'm scared if I answer you, saying you'll be undermining my job and what we've been doing for the past couple of years will be the most professional thing I can say to you,"

"I'm sorry," Sfiso said softly. "If I'm being truly honest with myself, I'm with her because a large part of me loves her and a small part of me that doesn't want to admit it is with her because she looks like Amanda,"

"This is what I want from you," Dr Woods said after a long while

3

Sfiso looked at his doctor intently before noting down his instructions and heading home. Finally, a place to calm down and relieve himself from the mess he'd just been through. The sooner he'd get to work, the better, because the longer he left it, the greater the chances of it being undone increased. With his homework done, it was time to treat his woman out to a special dinner as a way of saying sorry for all the shit that went down during what was now dubbed: Operation Pizza Night. The sound of keys rattling filled the house despite all the noise of a man cooking in the kitchen before Pinky's nosy head emerged into the kitchen.

"And then?"

"Surprise," Sfiso said with a half-hearted attempt at shock.

"Oh wow, really. You're not even trying to make an effort Sfiso,"

"I was, but you spoiled it by arriving early and being nosy, literally,"

Pinky shrugged in admittance, "Fair enough,"

"Now if you please, madam, if you would," he said, blindfolding his maiden and leading her towards a dark pre-load-shed dining room lit by nothing more than her favourite scented candles he'd stolen from the bathroom, and a glass of wine. Seconds later, he was back with dinner, roast chicken and vegetables. Not exactly romantic, but what made it so special was the fact that it was cooked via his hand and more importantly, burnt-free. Taking away her blindfold, her eyes were allowed to feast on the surprise that was prepared for her.

"Ncoah babe," she praised, wiping away an honorary tear at the effort her partner had gone through. "You did all this for me?"

"No, Satan's favourite cousin," he growled. "I'm glad you like it," he smiled, rubbing her hand.

"Are these my scented candles?" she shouted.

"Oops,"

"You're buying me a new set, I oath on my mother's grave, struu," crossing her fingers in irritation.

"Let's focus on the positive and not the negative," he giggled.

And that's what they did. Enjoying each other's company, tons of wine and plenty of drunken sex. This is what a relationship was meant to be like even when you'd fucked up and this is how you fixed things. Lots of communication and plenty of sex to cement things had changed for the better. One thing Sfiso wasn't ready to tell Pinky though, was his reason for seeing Doctor Green. Despite the love they shared, there were just some things love couldn't help with.

•••

The house was a mess, Pinky had a day off and had an unrelenting voice inside her telling her to clean the house, so why the hell not? It's not like her hubby would do it, after all, he was out off to the love of his life "Doctor Green". As their apartment got the make-over, it much deserved Pinky had to give it to Sfiso though, although he was no Bidvest or any other cleaning company the man knew how to keep the place clean, well, cleaner than she'd expected. His weaknesses, however, were dishes and ironing, something he could've avoided had he not gone to boarding school in her eyes. In her cleaning spree, she decided to go all out, changing curtains in their bedroom and even the sheets on their bed and that's when she saw the beginning of the end. As she flipped the bed and sheets hi-fived each other as they changed positions, she was startled by a letter that fell on the floor. It wasn't just any letter, had it been she would've returned it under the bed, but what caught her eye was her partner's handwriting and the strict words tattooed across the dead piece of wood:

Just Give It to Green!

What the hell did that mean? Was it a warning or a reminder, either way, nothing folded so delicately and hidden the way it had been could be denied that it was a secret? Was her man hiding things away from her already? The thought stung like 10 000 bees but if that was the game he wanted to play, then two could play it that way. She thought to herself as she gently and carefully opened the letter. What she read left her in awe as the more she read the harder she found it to read with her hand shaking with emotion but forced herself to finish and finish she did. The question was what now as she reread it...

... Amanda is getting married and nothing hurts more. Does this serve as definitive proof I haven't fully if ever gotten over her? I'm afraid to answer that question because of what it will do to the love and happiness it will do to the life I've created with Pinky...

Sfiso returned to a somewhat different home, none more so clear when he tried cuddling up to his woman at the end of the day, who remained cold and unresponsive. If there was any attempt on her part to hide how she'd felt, she had failed and hard. Despite all of her hubby's attempts to get her to warm up to him, she wouldn't budge. Truth be told, a part of her felt guilty about how her actions made him feel and, as a result, wanted to give Sfiso the benefit of the doubt, especially after all the hard work he'd put in trying to get her attention. But the harder and more devoted his attempts at trying to get attempts at any form of reciprocation of her love, the more she was reminded of that letter. The more it tore at her emotions and gave her the strength to carry on and keep him at arm's length. The perfect distance away from him ever getting another chance of hurting her in any shape, way, or form. More than anything else, this was a sign for her to move out and back to her own place, where any pain she inflicted would be self-inflicted.

And just as quickly as she had thought it, she was out of Sfiso's place, no longer able to refer to him as a partner or anything more like a lover because nobody who loved you would do what he had the audacity to do. Since the man was a lover of notes, that's what she would do, leave him a note telling him she'd moved out and ignored his calls the same way he had ignored her for who she truly was and seen her for the wrong reasons.

Home sweet home, as the saying goes. She'd moved out of her apartment for several reasons. The ones that stood out soon reunited themselves with her faster than she had time to unpack her bags. The constant sound of heavy-duty trucks moving up and down as they avoided the freeway to move shit about, the broken lift that had been out of order ever since Moses had split a river in two and the smell of piss on opposing staircases as she made her way up to the 5th floor. A place she was ashamed of until what she thought was the love of her life had taught her how to embrace it, despite her embarrassment and the fact it wasn't the best place to raise a child, it was home. But complaints aside, the first thing Pinky did was nap before waking up to an unrelenting knock on the door. 18 missed calls and so many unread WhatsApp messages her phone looked like it belonged to a teenage girl. She yanked the front door open in frustration to stop the unrelenting knocking only to find Sfiso and her baby boy, Lungelo standing there like police officers investigating a drug crime until the younger of the three shoved his way inside, dragging his luggage behind him.

Pinky looked at the two men shocked, before she realized Lungelo was meant to return from boarding school today. Given the number of missed calls on her phone, chances are her son had resorted to Plan B.

"Fuck," Pinky swore under her breath.

"I brought pizza," Sfiso shrugged, waving the box of her favourite pizza in her face before letting himself in.

"That was today?" she asked.

"Yesterday, but since you didn't pick him up, he decided to crash with me and because I don't want to go to jail, I still had to bring him back. Thank God I knew where you were. Thanks to the note you left," Sfiso faked a smile.

"You know I can still hear you two?" Lungelo mumbled. "Why are we back in this dump, anyway?"

"Baby boy, can you put your stuff in the other room, unpack and watch Netflix and let the adults speak for a bit, okay?"

"Hawu why? You still haven't even thanked Dad for bringing me here and I still want to find out why, that's what a dope lawyer would do," Lungelo cried with his arms in the air.

"Don't you ever call him that!" Pinky snapped. "This man will never be your father nor come close. So do as I say and stop being difficult,"

Lungelo looked at his father for any form of help with his mother's behaviour, raising an imaginary glass towards his lips before ducking a real one that shattered behind him.

"One more word from you and Imma kick your ass. I don't care how old you are," Pinky pointed.

"Listen," Sfiso said, approaching Lungelo gently. "For both our sakes, I think it's best you listen to your mother and do what she says or else your ass is not the only one that's going to get a beating. And besides, once I have all the answers, I'll be able to bring them all to you. Isn't that what a good legal assistant is supposed to do anyway?" he winked.

"But I didn't even say anything."

"This is not the time to be right. Just take my advice and thank me later," Sfiso said faintly, turning his son around and urging him to head towards his room. "Now where were we," he smiled, turning to face his girlfriend.

Pinky stared at Sfiso with her eyes unmoving. If anything, it looked like Sfiso was the one staring at her in an art gallery while she said nothing but watch as the two exchanged nothing other than a cosy moment of her doing.

"You," she growled.

"What?" he raised his eyebrows.

"What are you doing here?"

"Hawu, like I've said, I'm here to bring Lungelo,"

"Bring him or use him as an excuse to come see me since you miss your ex?"

"I'm confused,"

"Cut the bullshit Sfiso. We both know that you're only dating me because I remind you of her, nothing else,"

"That's not true,"

"I'm sure it must hurt. Especially now that she's getting married, knowing that the only way you'll ever get close to her is through me. No, wait," she said, tilting her head to the side. "You can't even do that cause not even her look-a-like wants you... ooh. Hows about that, being rejected by the original and the fake,"

"Pinky, whether or not you're sober, watch how you tread?"

"Or what, hmm? You can't throw me out, I've already moved back home and taken everything with me," she said, tapping the side of her head.

"You've conveniently seen what you want to see out of that blasted letter and yet you don't want to address the 'how we came about it in the first place. We wouldn't be having this conversation if it wasn't for your snooping around and-"

"So what, you're justifying this and blaming it on me by claiming I was snooping around and looking for something to fight about or better still, causing myself pain and suffering?"

"I didn't say that and yet you conveniently managed to skip over that point, even though it's written in black in white in that blasted letter of yours. Or how sure you've moved back to your own apartment but somehow conveniently seem to point out who's paying for your mother's medical aid or your son's school fees and now boarding fees because his mother just needs a little more time alone," Sfiso shrugged. "I may not be his father, but he definitely sees me as one because to me, he is my son. What's even better is the fact that you may be his parent but out of the two of us, I make the better one any day," clicking his tongue and grabbing his keys off the kitchenette beside the pizza and heading out the door. Leaving his words to fill in the presence he'd left behind.

Pinky sighed deeply before getting herself something with a percentage to drink and pouring herself an abnormally large glass of wine. After a long chug, she felt eyes on her and she was right. As she set the glass back down, she could face her son, who stood in the corner with eyes transfixed on her and presumably heard what had just happened. The two of them stared at each other in an unspoken competition, battling to see who would wink, let alone move first until Pinky gave in to her desires, taking another chug of wine, an act that rendered her son to turn back and like the tail of a leopard head back to the room from which he had once emerged.

4

Brenda was early for their coffee date which was unusually considerate of her considering the type of person she was and how her default answer was "Sorry I'm late" and as a result, it made Sfiso more anxious to meet with one of his best friends even though he had no reason to. But having overcome that fear the two friends sat down over a cup of coffee, and as the two individuals had a full-blown meal a few things made their way towards the light thanks to a full stomach. For starters, Sfiso's fight with Pinky was detailed and genuine in hopes of the most faithful and reliable feedback. To his credit, that's what he got, but it wasn't what he wanted to hear. As the woman with the freak out had a point, irrespective of how many times he'd pointed out that's what you get for snooping around. If Sfiso truly loved Pinky, then he wouldn't have to or be using her as a rebound for how he felt about Amanda, regardless of what his doctor had told him. If the shoe was on the other foot, this conversation wouldn't be happening over a pair of cleaned-out ribs and a half-finished cocktail but reinforced plexiglass at prison.

"Speaking of Amanda, how is she?"

"Smooth way to change the topic," Brenda shook her head. "She's getting married, how many emotions are there to choose from?"

"She's happy?"

"That's a rather redundant question don't you think?" Brenda asked, finishing her drink and asking a passing waitress for another. "Or do you mean, is she much happier now that you're no longer in the picture?"

"Yes," Sfiso whispered, dipping his head towards the ground and avoiding any form of eye contact.

"Very..."

Sfiso looked up at her with eyes bulging out.

"And there's your answer to why your girlfriend has every right to be angry at you," she said, pointing a straw at him. "As for my bestie. It's not my place to be airing out her dirty laundry because she confides in me and expects me to keep

16

my mouth shut. If the shoe was on the other foot, you'd expect me to do the same about how your relationship with Pinky works, well... supposedly works,"

"Fair enough, I get it," Sfiso said.

"Unless,"

"Ah shit, here we go. Unless what?"

"You know, I think another drink that is paid for will jog my memory on what's going on with Amanda," she said, scratching the bottom of her chin.

Three drinks later Brenda had one of two options, lie to one of her best friends or tell him the truth, regardless of either option she told him, he wouldn't be able to discern whether she was telling the truth because of her mental state but the look on his face. Whenever they brought up her name, it made it an extremely immense hurdle to jump over if she chose the former hurdle and if the truth ever came out, she would leap over it when the time came.

"So you want the good news or the bad news first?"

"Does it matter," Sfiso growled.

"Suit yourself," Brenda shrugged. "So the good news is that Amanda is getting married. Unfortunately, it isn't to you. What's even better news to hear for everybody sitting opposite that chair is that she's getting married to a doctor, a surgeon, no less. Can you imagine?" Brenda gasped.

"You don't say," Sfiso exclaimed, clicking his tongue.

"The flip side of that coin is that Amanda's mother's organs have packed up and left her. First, it was her kidney, which was okay, she only needs one. Her liver was next, doctors could save a chunk to keep things moving along but now her pancreas is applying for emigration and if it gets approved, that's it. The bouquets we'll be picking will be to throw over tombstones, not over crowds to see who's getting married next,"

"Why doesn't her husband help, he's a doctor, sorry, a surgeon after all?"

"I was waiting for you to say that. The only people who know of this are Amanda, her mother, me of course, and now you. If word gets out, it means there's only one place it could've come from and it ain't me,"

"But you just told me,"

"Those would be the same words Amanda would use if she knew about how you feel about Pinky, don't you think?" Brenda asked.

"Well, she was always one who hated sharing her emotions, I guess some things never change," Sfiso shrugged.

"There we go, now that sounds like a more appropriate response," Brenda smiled, raising her glass at him.

"So she's not with the doctor for his money or what he can do for her mother, but because she genuinely loves him?"

"Now even the answer to that question is beyond my superpowers," she finished, watching Sfiso withdraw to himself. "But there is one way to find out,"

"How?"

"Here," she said, passing a crumpled envelope.

"What's this?" he asked.

"Your invite to the wedding that you and your boo left behind when we were getting pizza,"

Sfiso grabbed the invite hesitantly before stuffing it into his pocket.

"Anyway, that's my cue. I have a wedding to plan. It was nice catching up," she said, standing up unsteadily and knocking over an empty glass. "Oops," she giggled. "Anyway, I hope to see you there. Imagine my best friend getting married and having my other best friend to share that moment with to make sure I wasn't just making it up,"

"Then you need to get some weed. That's less potent," Sfiso laughed. "Thank you," he smiled, kissing her on top of her forehead. "And we're getting you an Uber," he demanded. After watching her knock over drinks on an adjacent table as she tried to keep her balance.

5

With newfound clarity, Sfiso acted adjacent in attempt to get Pinky's attention. His attempts were no different to waves crashing in. In any other context, this would be deemed creepy, and the chances of him being in jail were strong. However, the fact it hadn't happened yet meant that Pinky's recognition of him and his attempts were high. The constant questioning from Lungelo of why he wouldn't let Sifiso through the door whenever he came to visit instead of letting him whimper inaudible messages outside like a bad voicemail made things worse. Eventually, she would crack and let the poor man in, not because she missed him or wanted anything from him, she'd moved on but due to a noise complaint. As for Sifiso, his unrelenting wavelike behaviour had let him get through the peer and now it was time to crash on the shore. All he needed was one moment, one last chance to prove himself, this would be a gamble where he bet all of his chips and he made sure she definitely knew that. For Pinky, this is not how she pictured how her breakup would be. She left Sifiso and returned to her old flat to live with her son uninterrupted. She moved on and he grovelled for her, not both men in her life ganging up on her for her attention whenever she didn't feel like giving it to either of them.

But she agreed to have dinner with him, which she shouldn't have because the news that she heard there changed her life forever. The love of her life wanted to start anew and get to know her for her and not for what or whom she'd seen her as. If need be, they could use the letter as a checklist of all the things he'd need to know, but still argued that would be a comparison, which to be honest was a fair argument. No secrets and no actions proved that statement more than what she considered nothing more than his date out with his supposed childhood friend than the wedding invite he slid across the table.

"She insisted I take it and said it was her whole reason for coming to see me in the first place, etc, etc," Sfiso explained.

Pinky nodded gently as she took it from him and placed it in her bag beside her purse and other valuables.

19

"Aren't you going to destroy it?"

"Is that what you want?" She asked.

"I mean, I thought that's what you were going to do," he said.

"That still doesn't answer my question,"

"Yes, let's. Together, so that no one can accuse the other of any suspicious behaviour, you know,"

"Okay, then that's what we're going to do" she smiled, squeezing both his hands spread across the table as they waited for dessert.

"Is there anything you want to tell me?" Sfiso joked.

"Yeah, I wanna baby," she laughed.

It didn't take long for the following weekend to come around, just a seven-day wait, and with it, it brought along the perfect weather to go out and enjoy a day out at the beach, which was a staple when one lived in a city renowned for its ocean. That, the Zulu culture and a stadium that was hardly used and had seen its glory days during a Soccer World Cup that had happened years ago. But amongst all of this, there was a couple that was on a mission to get to the edge of the peer and destroy a letter. It was a few pictures that would be left on social media and then the reason they were there in the first place as Pinky pulled out the wedding invite to Amanda Khoza and Boitumelo Molefe's wedding. They broke it into tiny pieces, too small to do anything with, and then Pinky let the pieces fly off, a gust of wind catching them and scattering them across the ocean. Whether the death of that invite did the same to the fish below because of the trash they'd just fed into an already polluted sea was no longer their problem as they smooched and spooned above before heading back home.

6

In Hollywood, the sight of your partner rolling over on top of you to cuddle you like a giant teddy bear appears to be romantic as fuck, but in reality, it couldn't be further from the truth. For starters, they are heavy, making it extremely hard to breathe, even more so if you're lying face down as though you're searching for a dropped cellphone rather than practising for being squeezed in a coffin. Then there's that dreaded morning breath that they don't seem to take into consideration and there's nothing romantic about that, even if it were to come from Beyonce herself. Something Pinky didn't take too kindly to when she heard Sfiso Say "Your breath stinks," and push her aside before clicking his tongue at her, angry at the fact that his sleep had been ruined.

"And then, what's your problem?"

"Nothing," he said.

"Nothing my ass. You can't tell me that bullshit when this supposed nothing was rocking your world leaving you out of breath," she said, moving her body like a belly-dancer.

"No really, it's nothing,"

"Then?"

"I would've preferred to wake up like a normal person," he sighed.

"And which way is that?" Pinky asked, raising her eyebrows.

"Any other way besides being crushed to death and having your morning breath all over my face,"

"So, in other words, you're trying to say I'm fat?"

"This is why I said it's nothing," Sfiso said before locking the bathroom door behind him and the sound of the shower filled the space between the pair of them.

•••

Lungelo helped his mother move the last bit of what was supposedly her mother's old clothes back into Sfiso's place, but old was a relative term, as they both knew she would simply buy new ones celebrating the occasion. It was finally a breath of fresh air to move and get away from that industrial area and move up to Pinetown. Sure, it wasn't five-star living, but three was sure better than one any day. This is where Lungelo would spend the remainder of his school holidays before he left, a place with wi-fi. But not everyone had a problem-free lifestyle to get accustomed to, and among Pinky's return. There were a few adjustments Sfiso had to get used to that he wasn't quite ready to accept, especially after having to live alone for such a long time. Like anybody sharing their living space, dishes were always a point of contention, which was something new because it wasn't a problem before she'd left the first time around, then there was Lungelo and the volume at which he constantly played the tv. It was a pet peeve more than anything but one he'd learn to adjust to, but the toilet lid was just a no. Toilet seat down. He didn't understand why? She didn't have a dick, so why did the lid have to come down all the time instead of just dropping it when she needed it? If she could answer that question for 10 marks, then he'd do it but she wouldn't, instead, she chose to start unnecessary fights about things that didn't matter and test the limits of what it meant to be in love. Peeing 365 times a day, constant nausea and always feeling tired. How? When you worked from home. But all that working from home meant that she got bored and eventually led to two types of news: good news and bad.

The good? Lungelo was finally going to have a younger sibling, news they'd strategically shared just before he'd returned to boarding school. The bad... swollen feet rendered Pinky useless, but it wasn't the only thing to swell up indefinitely. While they sent Sfiso on a mission to retrieve some foot cream to help with his partner's distress, shuffling about the messy drawer on her side of the bed, something caught his eye that couldn't be ignored, no matter how hard he tried. Despite Pinky's screams from the other side of the room for his return, he ignored them with expert precision as he focused all of his attention on the very same wedding invite that the both of them had destroyed. Whether it was an original or fake it didn't matter, the bigger question was... What was it doing there in the first place?

"Did you find it?" Pinky asked in relief.

"What the fuck is this?" Sfiso asked, waving the letter in the air.

"Ah shit," she sighed, dropping her head.

"That's all you have to say for yourself?"

"I can explain?" she said.

"Good, 'cause I'm waiting for an excellent explanation for this?" he said.

"Did you at least get the cream?" she asked.

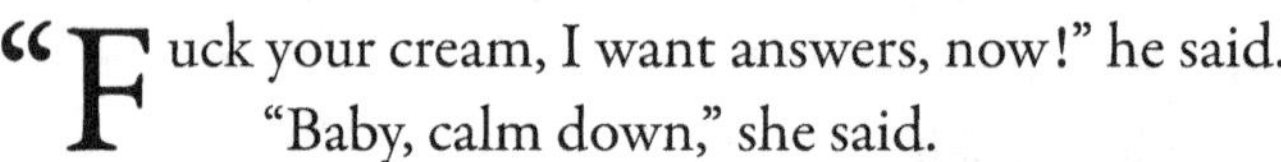

7

"Fuck your cream, I want answers, now!" he said.

"Baby, calm down," she said.

"I am calm, at least for now until I get my answers,"

Pinky sighed deeply as she studied her husband's body language. There was no talking to him reasonably in this state. She figured telling him the truth would only aggravate him even further, so the only option left was to do the only thing she could do.

"Well?"

"The truth is, I don't have an answer because I was under the intention you wouldn't find out, but it is what it is," she shrugged.

"Just as simple as that?" he said.

"Yes. As simple as that. As I said, I didn't think you'd find out, a matter of fact, you wouldn't have had you stayed in one place," she said.

"How many of these do you have left, in fact, an even better question to ask, why do you have this in the first place when we destroyed it. Together?!"

"That's the only one left. I had my reasons, chief among them was just in case I need to see our ex," she said, rolling her eyes.

"Reasons, you have reasons for this?" he said, waving the invite around.

"You. You won't understand," she said. "I don't expect you to," she finished, getting up from the couch. "What I do know now is what comes out of that mouth now will be nothing but a, 'I need you to believe this. I meant everything I said on that peer,'" she said, standing in front of him, trying to grab the invite from him.

"Not so fast smooth mouth. I don't care whether you meant it or not. What you need to know now is that as long as you are in my house. Making me second-guess everything that comes out of your mouth even if the facts are right there in front of me is a no-no. Understood," he said. "I just can't seem to understand why you couldn't just tell me. Why you went to such extensive lengths in order to keep this from me and if things turned out your way, how

24

things would've panned out? The more I think about it, the more questions come up that I can't seem to answer," Sfiso said softly before turning on his foot. "They say actions speak louder than words and if this is your way of showing a glimpse of how you express those actions, then..."

"Are you done?" she sighed.

"Yes," he said, turning his back to her and walking away.

She watched him walk away and then went to the kitchen to get the foot cream he was supposed to get.

BRENDA WAS BACK IN KZN on wedding duties and like any good wedding planner, kept her planning secrets to herself. Secrets she found out the hard way accompanied by a lack of transparencies, were the worst. What she didn't intend was for her best friend to agree to meet her and help her with some of her errands so easily when Sfiso was renowned for being difficult, but who was she to say no to help when she was being given it. Besides, every time she came down to the coast it had changed drastically, almost as if to give her the middle finger for moving away, highlighting the fact that she wasn't from the province even further. And so there they were, dashing for flowers in the north and Egyptian cotton in the south.

"Oooh, there's something I need to show you," Brenda cooed.

"Take a picture, I'm sure it'll be just as epic, speaking of which, it's time for me to head home," Sfiso said.

"You can't do that, it'll ruin my surprise," she said.

"Life is full of surprises" Sfiso shrugged before looking for the N3.

"And I've got one for you if you decide to listen to me for once and go out to dinner with me,"

"Nothing new there," he said.

"What's new is I want you to bring Pinky along," Brenda smiled.

"What?" Sfiso said in conjunction with the control of the car as it stop swerving from his shocked reaction.

"You heard me, and there's no way I'm repeating myself after what just happened. This time around, you might crash for real," Brenda snubbed.

"Why?" he asked.

"If I tell you it'll defeat the whole point of it being a surprise, won't it?" she said, clicking her tongue.

As the two drove back to Pinetown, they informed Pinky of their intentions and prepared her beforehand, despite all of her questioning. Sfiso could only inform her as much as he knew, which wasn't much, leading to a self-destructive circle.

8

The trio spilt over into the lobby of a hotel that was further north and the couple accompanying Brenda knew that something fishy was up. Alas, they'd made it this far and continued to follow along, their body language saying one thing while their mouths said another. The hotel restaurant allowed for a complex mix of feelings as Brenda eagerly introduced Amanda and her soon-to-be husband to Pinky and Sfiso. All Brenda needed now was a chair that reclined and some popcorn to watch the response Amanda gave to Pinky and Sfiso gave to Amanda. The awkwardness didn't last as long as everybody expected, thanks in part to the bride's friend who had planned for this. As the night dragged on, alcohol brought out a side of the bride and Sfiso that they were working hard to hide from everybody else. The two began re-enacting what going out with Brenda back in varsity was like, as she was still sober enough to hover over them and keep a watchful eye over them. All a husband-to-be could do was watch intently and have a glimpse at his wife. If that's what Amanda was to Sfiso, to begin with, all he could do was watch and take notes on how to do it should things turn south.

"So how long have you guys been together?" Pinky asked, diverting her attention from her own man to the one in front of her.

"Close to a year, give or take," the surgeon shrugged.

"Wow, that's really accurate for a surgeon, don't you think?"

"I know right," he said, raising his hands to his cheek in dramatic shock.

"I can see why you guys are so perfect for each other," Pinky smiled.

"Hmm?" Boitumelo responded, looking up from his phone.

"Nevermind,"

As the night proceeded, the number of sober people dwindled until all that was left was Boitumelo and Pinky, who herself ended up succumbing to the elements around her. Whether this was out of genuine interest or not, it didn't matter as the lady of the night was overcome with a sheer amount of jealousy at the amount of attention her fiancé was receiving. Irrespective of how she looked like she'd crossed the socializing and catching up bridge with Sfiso a century ago. To an unbeknownst pair of eyes, tasked with allocating the job of groom and surgeon along with visitors, the titles would be mixed up, but now with everybody separated and heading off to their designated sleeping areas, it was left to Brenda to convince Sfiso that he was too drunk to drive home and needed to sleep over. Fact was, he didn't and as glowing as that made Pinky on the inside, the reality of the situation was that they needed to face the truth which was unfortunate because Brenda was right. Even if she didn't like her, she couldn't disagree with her, they were in no condition to drive home and she was too tired to wait until she sobered up. So, she just wanted to find a bed and go to bed. Just like that, with her chanting at the back of what was going to happen, it was the end of the night, including for Sfiso.

9

Whether it was 'what's her face... Brenda or doctor', it didn't matter. All that did matter was how grateful she was for their level-headedness. Who knows what could've happened if she and Sfiso were on the road and something happened. She couldn't bare the thought of leaving her son behind, let alone come to terms with the fact that all the actions that led to that would be of her own doing. Speaking of Sfiso, the familiar but annoyable sound of him snoring filled the room, making her dread waking up first, reminding her of the headache that came with drinking too much clear alcohol the night before. There were two ways to put a stop to all of this, get up and try to start her day or put a pillow over the man's mouth. It would make sense given everything he'd put her through emotionally so far and what she'd seen with her own eyes yesterday. The man could sell the cold to a block of ice, it's often said actions speak louder than words but no word could defeat "wow" from what she saw yesterday. Right now she needed a cold shower or was it a hot one like the surgeon said. She couldn't remember. Pinky laughed at her own joke as she quickly googled for the answer, something she wouldn't have to do if the doctor was around to tell her. With the internet done with its task she stumbled over to her luggage to get her things, well, what was supposed to be her bag before realising it wasn't hers to begin with. With Sfiso's bag now closed, she opened her own and continued with her mission of having a shower, which she now knew had to be warm.

Whether it was already time to wake up or the sound of water in the shower, it took him a while to register what was going on, but his mind returned fast when he remembered what happened last night. Honestly speaking, the doctor seemed like a pretty chilled guy and there was nothing to be worried about. Whether there was a reason to or not, he'd crossed that bridge a long time ago and had new ones to build. Pinky emerged from the bathroom and nothing made him lazier to get up than the fact that he'd have to be next. Banging on the door startled the both of them, however, between the two, Pinky was able to hide hers better. It continued like police in movies before they broke down the door, throwing away any doubts of it being hotel staff.

"Coming!" Pinky shouted. She looked at Sfiso and gestured for him to attend to the door.

"You're the one who said you're going, go," he whispered.

"You're the man," she said.

"I'm naked," he said.

"Here's a towel," she said, throwing hers at him.

"What's taking you guys so long" Brenda shouted from the other side of the door.

"Your best friend," Pinky said, quickly trying to decide on whether she should wear jeggings or a jean.

Brenda appeared around the corner, visibly obvious that she'd let herself in. She stared around the room replicating a fascinated tourist at Table Mountain getting ready to take pictures. "You guys are so late, why aren't you dressed? We're going out for breakfast, so look decent, no sneakers and look like a rap star you always try to pull off. You're 30 now, act your age," she said, pointing at Sfiso, who had nothing but a towel wrapped around his waist. "Girl, pick the jeans, leggings will cause drama. Not everybody has recovered from last night. I've heard I got a headache one too many times," she pointed. "The last thing I need is talking over people's asses when this is over. I've got my own problems to deal with when all of this is finished," she sighed. "I hate it when someone tells me what to wear but because of your figure, I'd choose the blouse but again, I'll leave that all to you as long as you come in jeans and..." looking at her smartwatch, 15 minutes because this one," pointing at Sfiso, "Still has an issue with time,"

And as just as quickly as she had appeared she was gone, a real-life fairy godmother so to speak. And so, just as she had spoken, let her will be done in under 15 minutes. Further downstairs, the trio waited in the lobby for the remaining duo that held them up talking about the upcoming wedding to pass the time. For something that's always said to be small, it sure had a lot of must-haves. 15 minutes later, Sifiso and Pinky revealed themselves in the lobby and the five of them disappeared into the car park and into Pinky's dream car, Amanda's new Range Rover.

"Sorry guys, I'm not sitting in that middle chair, I'm not five, I'd rather be on my own here in the back, besides it'll do me a lot of good," Brenda waved jumping into the third row of seats.

Pinky's heart rate needed attending to, and Sfiso had to decide whether he needed to stop his ex from acting like an idiot or just let herself go ahead because nobody knew how she felt about this car except him. Nobody understood it, but the best way to describe it was close to receiving money when you didn't expect it, no... it was bigger than that. No, a teenager without their phone, forced to live without social media and learn to re-establish themselves in the community. That's more like it. This was Pinky's dilemma, squeezing Sfiso's hand tightly as a way of reassuring herself that this was real, biting her lip to stop herself from screaming. With all the features for her to devour even closer, Pinky enjoyed them while they lasted, acting out of place and more like a football-crazed football fan.

"We're here," Sfiso said, forcing Pinky out of the car.

Sfiso watched in silence as Pinky gazed at his ex's fiancé, technically he could do nothing about it but it did make him feel uncomfortable. It got on his nerves and the best way to control his emotions was to do what they had come here to do in the first place, eat.

"Everything okay?" Brenda asked, yanking her friend away from everybody to make it look like she needed help getting out of the car.

"Yes, it is why?"

"You've behaved this entire trip even when you and Amanda were drunk and that, my friend, is very out of character of you," she said in a soft voice.

"People change," Sfiso shrugged.

"Yes, video game characters. I've got a better chance of being the next person to get married between the both of us and I don't even have a partner," she said.

"Like I said, nothing. You're just seeing things as usual, that's all," Sfiso sighed.

"Being part of this is fucked up as it is, I know I'm trying to understand it in my own special way, how you haven't stabbed the groom or have me rescue you from jail after professing your undying love to your ex is a miracle. Clearly, you paid somebody who looks like you to come do this, anyway, let's go. We're holding everybody up," Brenda said, squinting at him while they walked to join everybody else.

"Like I said, people change, we all have our reasons why we're here," he smiled.

10

If it wasn't eggs baked in goat's cheese or pancakes with names he couldn't pronounce, it was chocolate on food where it shouldn't be but regardless, from this point onwards, they'd never come a point in Sfiso's life where he'd be told he hadn't eaten a certain type of food. As for everybody else on the table, your standard English breakfast was enough except for Brenda, who was willing to try Swedish cinnamon buns because they looked funny. Other than that, there was nothing special about the venue except for the cool sea breeze in the morning.

"So Sfiso, any tips on how to keep a woman like Amanda happy?" Boitumelo Joked. "I'm sure you're the best person to ask"

"Me? There's Brenda right there," pointing across the table, "What the hell do I know about keeping Amanda happy?"

"No...Happy," Boitumelo grinned.

"Ayi Wena," Amanda scolded, slapping her fiancé across the arm.

"To be honest with you, I can't remember it's been that long," he said, staring down Pinky "And besides, not to sound rude or anything but I've been with people who've made me forget about your fiancé's preferences in the bedroom, sorry chief,"

"You wish you could forget about me," Amanda said, snapping her fingers back and forth at him. "I rocked your world,"

"Sorry, can I please get another refill on the cappuccino and another one to go, cinnamon buns and the bill please, thank you," Brenda asked while their waiter scribbled down her request.

"And what does that mean, exactly?" Boitumelo asked.

"You stole the words right out of my mouth," Pinky added, placing her cup down on the table.

"He knows what I mean," she said.

"But I don't and would like to. After all, if you can rock his world and make it unforgettable by I assume being on your knees, why can't I enjoy the same, is it because I've been on one and him none?" Boitumelo asked.

"Then how does she mean it, since you apparently know the answer?" Pinky demanded, her body and attention now invested in Sifiso.

"As I said, I've been with other people in the bedroom. I'm no Casanova but they've done things to me and I'm sorry to say this about your wife," looking at Boitumelo. "Taking her completely out of the picture and if she still feels like she rocked my world, that's on her. I've been with women who've taken me to other galaxies, let alone planets, and kudos to them," Sifiso shrugged.

"You're going to tell us who those women are," Pinky demanded.

"No," he said.

"Hmm, ok"

"Thank you," Brenda nodded, accepting the bill as they began to clean up and gently handed it over to Boitumelo who sighed and waved her off in irritation, his attention focused on what was in front of him and trying to avoid any distractions.

"Are you going to tell me all the men you've ever slept with?" Sfiso asked.

"No, because this is not about me," Pinky said.

"That and it would be a pretty long list. So, if you're not willing to share your till slip of men, why am I being forced to ruin the privacy of all the women I've ever slept with? Just because you did it to her, and she enjoyed it doesn't mean it'll work for all of them. And if you really want to know whether your wife is good at sex or not, ask her not me, you're a doctor aren't you?" Sifiso said, standing up and taking one of Brenda's cinnamon buns.

"I was going to eat that," she protested.

Pinky jumped from her chair in frustration and followed Sifiso demanding answers from him. Her past might have been plotted with mistakes but it didn't give him the authority to play around with her. For example, the letter was a great example of him making a mistake and her being the bigger person. "Ah shit, the letter," she said, remembering its existence.

"And where do you think you're going? Calm down," Brenda snatched almost knocking her off her balance.

"Get off me, bitch, my man need's me, not that you'd know anything about that," Pinky said, dusting herself off as she looked Brenda up and down.

"Man, boyfriend, husband, you two call each other different names more times than a baby changes its nappy."

"It's complicated,"

"It's bound to be if neither of you don't know what's going on between each other,"

"Just stay out of Sifiso and I's business. We came here for a wedding apparently, we don't need to add a funeral either I've got a busy schedule," Pinky said clicking her tongue at her.

"But she's right, it really isn't that complicated. If there's something wrong between you two, fix it now before it becomes a problem, avoiding it will only make it worse," Amanda sighed.

"And you know this because you're a master on the subject especially when it comes to your ex's feelings don't you?" Boitumelo remarked.

"I don't know why we're having this discussion now and why he threatens you all of a sudden when you're the one who insisted we do this," Amanda heaved, throwing her arms towards the floor from the sky.

"I wasn't the one hiding how I rocked people's worlds,"

"Who told you to start mining in tunnels you weren't supposed to be digging in the first place? If you had insecurities about making me happy in the bedroom then that's where you should've asked, not blast it on live social media and try see how many likes you'd get for it, unfortunately, life isn't built that way,"

"Guys, I think it's best we head back, I'll fetch the far, Amanda, keys?" Brenda insisted.

Everybody followed her instruction as they were herded into the SUV without objection. The next problem was where to from here, but Amanda was right, all these people needed to sort out their problems at the hotel not here, also, she'd get a break from being a referee to all the fighting that was going on and just enjoy what was left of her cinnamon buns and Cupachinno.

I t was quiet all round, either Sifiso and crew had checked out without saying
goodbye, had checked out but still around to enjoy the hotel's hospitality for
as long as they could before they left or the least likely option had booked again
and were now staying in a different room, either way, Brenda was able to catch up
with her bestie at the bar having a drink and watching whatever was on tv but his
mind completely elsewhere.

"I should've tried the pancakes as well, I'm craving them now that I've
finished the buns,"

"At least now you'll be willing to try something new," Sifiso smiled.

"Speaking of new things, do you want to talk about what happened at
breakfast?"

"Nope"

"Okay," she said rubbing his back.

With luggage on either side of her arm, Pinky was ready to finally leave, it
was fun indeed but it was time to face the truth and the truth is they couldn't
stay there forever and more importantly, she missed her son. With her mind
elsewhere it was brought back to reality by crashing into a wet, sweat-covered
Boitumelo who was from an intense gym session or run. His glistening skin
highlighting his toned physique even further.

"Sorry about that, I didn't see you, I must be dizzy from all that lifting, I guess
I need to sit down."

"No, no, no, it's fine, I need to pay more attention to where I was going so
thanks," Pinky smiled.

"Who kicked you out, what's with all the bags?" Boitumelo joked.

"No, we're actually going back home, the babysitter needs to leave plus I miss
my son," Pinky smiled.

"How motherly of you. At least let me help you carry that down to the lobby,
consider it a goodbye gesture," Boitumelo smiled.

"Thanks, oh, and before I forget. This is for you," she said handing him an envelope out of her vest.

"Oh no it's fine, I don't need any financial reward," he smiled, pushing the envelope away. "I'm doing this out of the goodness of my heart,"

"Read it whenever you have time alone,"

"What is this?" Waving the letter around.

"You'll find out when you read it, the thing is, I don't know much about your wedding preparations with your fiancé but this might help," She smiled.

"Thanks,"

"Don't mention it," she nodded. Bemused herself before seeing the image of her man having her back rubbed by some bitch that just wouldn't seem to go away ever since she revealed her face. She was like a fly on traditional meat, irritating and indecent.

"Ready," Pinky said clearing her throat startling both of them.

"Let's go then," Sifiso advised jumping off his chair and asking for the bill for his drink.

"See you around then, don't worry, I'll pay for it" Brenda insisted watching them walk out of the hotel before turning to attend to the bill. "Fuck! How many drinks did this guy have?"

11

As any mother would tell you, in fact, any adult would tell you, getting back from work and still having to cook supper is one of the most degrading things that can happen to you, especially if you have more than one mouth to feed. Lungelo laid on the couch, despite the number of times being told not to lie on it but to sit like it was created for. Pinky was simply tired of repeating herself, telling him the same thing over and over, as though the boy had an extreme case of Alzheimer's. She refused to be distracted by her phone and imitate her son but ever since their... trip, she'd developed a new habit of checking it now and again like a person expecting an answer from a potentially successful job interview and it's not like Sifio's return from work changed anything other than the way Lungelo sat on the sofa. Pinky didn't like how things had turned out, how her son had more respect for him than her which was strange but she had to face the truth, she'd never find this kind of behaviour anywhere else even if Lungelo's biological father appeared from the other side of that door right now. She'd wait for the supposed fixer of all these teenage problems she had to put up with to finish dishing up and get comfortable before addressing what was on her mind.

"We need to address some things, some of which I think highlighted themselves when you saw Amanda and without dear, I say it, Brenda's help could've sent things down a different road," Pinky said.

"Ah fuck, here we go," Sifiso said.

"Hey, language," Lungelo reprimanded.

"And if you don't want to hear more, I suggest this you go to your room," Pinky told him.

"But I'm not allowed to eat in my room,"

"I'll make an exception for tonight," she pointed.

Lungelo swore under his breath as he left the lounge and headed towards his room knowing he was about to miss out on something juicy that was about to happen when his parents weren't shouting at each other and wanted to talk it often meant something big was going to happen. With Lungelo gone, Pinky was now free to let her feelings flow uninhibited.

"So... what is it, that you want to tell me?" Sifiso asked.

"What exactly is this? What do you call this relationship, because it is one... it just doesn't have one and if it does, I just don't know the name?"

"I don't think I understand," he said

"Oh, you understand me very well, is this a friendship, relationship or like I said one you've given a name but haven't told me about, and if this is a relationship, what am I to you because unfortunately, I am not interchangeable like a Rubik's cube,"

Sifiso said nothing.

"Your silence speaks more than any words you could've given me, thank you for answering my question," she said, taking his empty plate and going to the kitchen.

"Look," chasing after her. "After saying this, maybe I should move out, even though it's my place. The freckles on your face and the fact that I now have a son I love more than anything even though when we first met I preached how much I wasn't ready for a child only to find out it was because you wanted to drop the bomb that part of your past. You're right, as always. Going out and giving in to Brenda's insistence showed some things I was planning to keep hidden forever. But if it's the truth you want, then here it is. When we first started dating it was to heal the pain Amanda had caused me because of the similar features you guys share. But the more I was with you the more I realised how much of a different person you were and you taught me to love you for you and not who I wanted you to be. That's what I think explains a lot of the fighting and unnecessary breaking up and making up back and forth. For that, I'm sorry, even though it won't fix the pain it caused,"

"Impressive speech," Pinky said, pausing to give him a fake smile before returning to the cutlery in the sink.

"What?"

"Impressive speech, but tell that bullshit to someone else, not me,"

"But I..."

"When you're sober maybe, but when you're drunk and in front of the woman you yourself just admitted you can't get over, then it's a different story. She said.

"Meaning?" He asked, confused.

"Meaning, the both of you still aren't over each other but refuse to admit it,"

"What do I have to do to prove to you that I no longer have feelings for that woman and have moved on? I love you, despite my mistakes,"

Pinky finished the dishes, seemingly ignoring Sifiso's confession, who waited anxiously as she finished restoring the dinnerware in its proper place.

"As I said, it's a brilliant speech, but it still hasn't answered my question of what we are. If you love me like you claim you do, then the answer to that question is simple. Don't go,"

"Okay," he nodded.

"Just like that?"

"Just like that," he repeated.

12

She shoulder charged him as she left the kitchen, checking her phone before heading into the bedroom. Sfiso followed her, laying in the opposite direction while she performed her daily preparations before bed. Pinky's phone rang and she hesitantly answered it after ogling at the caller ID. There was only one person since she knew of Sifiso's existence that she hated more than Amanda and that was Thabile. The proud owner of that name belonged to his mother. Who, when push came to shove, was a competition of who hated one more than the other, irrespective of trying to at least put their differences aside for Sifiso. She watched her phone ring, wondering what she wanted and why she could call her of all people, when her son was right beside her. Despite her better judgement, she answered the phone.

She kept her mouth closed and listened to what the precursor to another generation of lying had to say. If she was a normal mother, she would've simply told her to tell Sifiso to call her when he was available. She didn't want to tell him that she was ill, as this would create a lot of strain, as everyone knew how Thabile and she didn't get along. It would be difficult to explain why she found out about her illness before him, especially with Sifiso having faith in whatever his mother said, even if it was something crazy, like the earth was flat. As bad as the news was though, a small part of her soul made her dimples go to work before drifting off to sleep until the sound of her phone woke her up.

"Hello," she spat.

"Hello, can I please speak to a Miss Pinky Khumalo"

"Who's asking? It's late, they can leave a message,"

"Oh sorry, that's also an option, that totally slipped my mind," he thought out loud. "Please tell her that Dr Molefe called,"

"Hey," she said, jumping out of bed. "To what do I owe this surprise so late,"

"Sorry to disturb you so late. I just realised the time, sorry,"

"Ag, there's nothing to be worried about when you save lives, you're bound to finish late now and again," she said, waving him off with her other hand.

"I'm calling to just say thank you,"

"Thank you?" Pinky said confused.

"For the letter. It explained a lot and cleared up a lot of confusion for me, especially after this trip Amanda had insisted on,"

"Oh,"

"So now that I know what's going on I've got nothing to fear about my marriage I no longer see your partner as a threat as he is not the problem I need to deal with but that being said I do that have a problem I need to solve before my marriage in order to have a long and happy one that will last as long as possible,"

"What?"

The two talked for a while or to put it into context, for as long as it took to wait in the doctor's office.

"Hey Doctor, not all of us have our own businesses. Some of us have to get up in the morning, which is basically over," she shrugged.

He laughed and said goodbye and she went back to sleep, which wasn't for long before Sifiso woke up. A man who wasn't particularly quiet during his morning routine. She woke up annoyed and watched him get ready for his day like it was the first time, the two said nothing to each other despite the constant looks in each other's direction before Pinky remembered the news she was told last night. She repeated it to Sifiso as he left the bedroom, trailing behind him to make breakfast for Lungelo before he went off to school.

Pinky was now left alone in silence with her thoughts as she threw herself on the couch and let it sound like a silent fart as it took on her weight. The silence around her felt unspoilt, giving her the proper platform to evaluate the conversations that took part yesterday. Thabile, even though there was nothing bright about her, was ill, it was clearly not the flu since they ended up calling her and not Sifiso about it. Whether she was the intention out of fear of breaking the news to her son or an honest mistake because of the time, however, the odds of the latter were unlikely. Her phone rang, startling her and bringing her back to reality. It surprised her to find out it was a call from Boitumelo but took it in her stride, what else could surprise her at this point given all that had happened in the last 24 hours?

"Hey, to what do I owe this unexpected surprised," Pinky blushed.

"What, two friends can't call each other?"

"Oh, we're friends now?" Pinky asked.

"Well, I believe that's how most friendships start, no?" he said.

"Most of mine start over a drink and unfortunately there is none, so..."

"That can be arranged," Boitumelo laughed.

The two talked and laughed with one another until the real reason for the two-hour-long phone call surfaced.

"I think my fiancé is cheating on me with her ex, or at the very least still hasn't gotten over her. Problem is, I can't find the strength to leave her even if that's true,"

"What makes you say that?" Pinky said softly.

"Because she won't get married unless Sifiso is present,"

13

The words echoed through her head as though it were nothing but an empty cave. How could Boitumelo put up with this, what? How could she put up with this, after everything that had happened thus far this was the hardest blow administered to her. Granted Sifiso had changed and was supposedly making a genuine effort to prove that but this was still his past and if she was a window that brought light into his future then this curtain was having none of it but she was human and no matter how much she told herself that she loved him there was only so much she could take.

Lungelo was surprised to find her mother waiting for her as soon as he finished school, sure he had plans of his own but the odd sighting of his mother's car as he walked towards the taxi rank with his friends meant there was not much he could do. He knocked on the window startling her in the process as she opened it for him to enter before kicking the car to life.

"Hawu, and then?"

"Hello to you too," shaking her head.

"No, it's not that. It's just that I'm surprised to see you here, if it was dad coming to pick me up, yeah sure but you..." he shrugged.

"And I've got a surprise for you," she said after some time, navigating her way through the after-school traffic. It was a Friday, Lungelo could be in uniform for so long as they spread themselves across the city and Pinky using her son to avoid home and Sifiso via him. So it was a trip to the mall for a pair of new attire and the perfect time for the two to get reacquainted with no strings attached. No talk about school and what to study once Lungelo was done with matric, just a genuine update on his son's interests and trying to get a firm grasp and understanding of what the fuck was wrong with this generation. Pinky had figured out his son's sexuality a long time ago but dared not to bring it up until he was comfortable too, which was fine, which was how it was supposed to be but on the other side of the table. Lungelo felt tormented, unable to decide if this was the right time to tell her if they'd be a right time to tell and how he should tell her.

After all, this is how white parents did things not black, however, that statement was the worst thing he'd said to himself and hurt more than any homophobic comment that had and was yet to come his way.

"Ma,"

"Hmm," she hummed, while she furiously typed on her phone.

"I want to tell you something but please don't judge me or hate me, okay,"

"I'd never do that, you're my baby," she said, placing her phone down and giving him her full attention.

"I'm gay," he said after a long while and a deep breath.

"And I'm glad you're happy,"

"No, Ma. You don't understand, I'm attracted to men,"

"And like I said, I'm happy for you," she said, placing his hands in hers.

"I don't think you're taking me seriously," he said, snatching them away and clicking his tongue. "This is why I never tell you anything,"

"And I'm surprised that you don't know what the meaning of gay means even though you're throwing it around so much. As I said, I'm happy for you, just don't bring around some tattooed brawler of a man with nothing but gold teeth and fresh out of jail when you come introduce 'the one', please spare me the heartache," she said raising her hands in the air.

Lungelo rolled his eyes in agreement. As the night wore on he began to wonder when they'd head back home, it wasn't like his mother to stay out "this late" unless at a family gathering or with friends but it seems he'd spoken too soon as a few of his mom's friends joined them, ultimately putting an end to their day out together. The nail in the coffin being given money to go watch a movie while the grown-ups talked for a bit and then they'd go home. As the two made their way apart like the splits, in so doing they exchanged emotions, momentary happiness on one side and inexplicable sadness on the other as it disappeared towards the movie theatre.

Pinky didn't expect her friends to arrive early, it was out of character. She was on the phone confirming details about their arrival while discussing her son's sexuality and then boom, they were here. Her son had found someone to vent out his problems and so now it was her turn but in order for her to loosen up they needed some drinks, plus it would keep the vibe going until Lwazi joined them, which was a trait that she was used to. They could only have so many long islands before Tumi convinced them to find a place better suited for their needs, they couldn't wander off too far due to Lungelo but they found themselves a bar down the road where three drinks turned to four and four turned to six. Several missed calls later Lungelo was put on voicemail every time he tried calling his mother and out of data, he bumped into Lwazi or Aunty Lwazi as tradition would dictate who was looking for his mother, after a brief update of what had happened she tried calling Pinky only to be put on voicemail herself, as odd as it was for Pinky not to answer the phone she was able to locate her by calling other's she was supposed to meet with. With Lungelo at her heels, the two were able to locate her drink high in the air before chugging it down as though it were flavoured water before twerking and wooing a gathering crowded around her, spurred on by her friends who were slapping her ass. Lungelo watched frozen, getting a first-hand glimpse of the evils that lay ahead in university in just a few determining papers away. Like a gargoyle ignored by everybody, he was able to watch unhindered as Aunt'Lwazi dragged his mother around the collar of her neck like a sack of potatoes towards the door much to the booing of the packed bar, her idol sliding along the floor, putting up a fight at first but too drunk to do so, the only remnants of her presence being heels left behind like spilt over vegetables. At this point, you wouldn't even be able to point out Tumi and the others even if your winnings of the lotto depended on it but that mattered little for Lungelo was behind Lwazi and his mother with the execution of a shut of shut door.

"Stay here, and watch over her," Lwazi ordered, laying Pinky on the side of the road in what seemed as though was a hooker high on meth.

Lungelo nodded and not long after she was gone, Lwazi was back and they crammed his mother into her car and drove off. She was too drunk to go home and at this point didn't even remember her own name. Once at Lwazi's, Pinky was laid to rest in the guest bedroom and Lungelo sat down with his saviour over a plate of spinach and chicken feet.

14

Full, he could focus his attention on other things happening around him and seeing his mother taken over by liquid courage was not one of them. The thought of taking over a drunk mother wasn't something new for anybody his age, but it was behaviour that was completely out of character. As neither Lungelo nor Pinky spoke up, speaking about it never arose. Lungelo and his aunt sat at the coffee table, taking advantage of the time that passed between them while waiting for dinner to arrive. He watched in silence while she prepared whatever secret concoction his aunt made to keep his mother sane before and he feigning attending to his school books.

"It sucks, doesn't it?"

"Huh?" Lwazi asked, confused.

"No matter how many times you walk in there; she doesn't seem to get better?" Lungelo said softly, chewing on his pen.

Lwazi looked onward convincingly, trying to dispel any confusion created by her best friend's offspring. The two continued to sit in awkward silence.

"Although I know mom isn't an alcoholic, the thing that has been bothering her has made her return to drinking, though she has been trying to keep me in the dark."

"What makes you say that?" Lwazi asked with eyebrows raised high enough to start an argument on whether they were drawn.

"She's just decided to drink, out of the blue. Whatever is bothering her, she thinks she can drink it away. It clearly seems to be working for her because she gets to drink, not remember who her name is, sleep, wake up the next day and get to do it all over again. Which is kinda unfair because she's supposed to be my mother, not the other way around. There are only so many times I can put her to bed,"

"How would you like me to help?" she asked.

"Well, for starters, I'd like for my parents to stop fighting because it's turning them into alcoholics. If that can't happen, then I'd like whatever that can happen to happen as long as I don't have to take her to AA meetings,"

"I see," she said before the two of them stewed in a pile of awkward silence. "So when do I get to meet the lady that's going to steal you from me?" she asked after a while, trying to fill the void filled by the silence between them.

"And what makes you think it's a lady, what if it's a man... what then?" he asked.

"I'll need a Plan B in case my designer bags and earrings don't work as a bribe," she said.

•••

When Pinky awoke the next morning, it was as if nothing had happened. She rushed her son for wasting time, all the while she wanted to leave and return back to her abode... for his sake. It was kind of Lwazi for her to take care of her and Lungelo the way she had for the past several hours, but she was a grown woman and could take care of herself on her own. Eventually, she made it out of her friend's house and was back in her own home, able to celebrate her freedom in peace. As much as she didn't like drinking it at least made her be honest with herself and the reality she found herself in. She ordered another drink and the realization with it as it soothed her parched throat that the place she called home was nothing more than a mere house as the person whose name was on the lease's heart was elsewhere, only for the gap to be filled by her own, which now left a cavity that made for a really cool vodka fountain. The only person who could understand her pain regardless was getting married to the source of her pain. When it came down to it, there was one common denominator. She stood up, dizzy, paid for her drink before buying everybody else a round. How she got home that night is between God, the bartender, and the Uber driver who drove her home. Any normal person would be thankful and use the experience as a means to turn a new leaf but for Pinky it was a sign to get a new makeover. First her hair and then her wardrobe and even though it got her attention it ended up making her feel even worse. The things that were meant to make her feel better and make her forget about the pain caused by Sifiso were only highlighted by the fact that they were noticed by Boitumelo. She couldn't understand why it bothered her so much when the answer was so simple and she'd already decided. Sifiso's ex wouldn't get married without him attending, it wasn't a decision for her to make but one for Boitumelo to decide and of course. The unforgettable day when he decided to sit her down and explain that he was worried about her, how she was acting out of character and the ripple effect it caused. She had to fight the urge to lash out when being lectured about thinking about the feelings of others and the reason this conversation happened in the first place was because of him. It didn't matter how many no's were said, Sfiso was still going to that wedding, the question was... would everybody on the other side give a thumbs up?

15

Amanda came home and threw whatever she thought she'd need last minute on the floor as shopping bags crunched beneath her, imitating her as she threw herself on the sofa. She let out a dramatic sigh and Boitumelo continued to watch television despite the loud interruption. "Babe,"

"Hmm," he said, his eyes still fixed on the tv.

"You won't believe what happened to me today," she said, adjusting herself in order to spill out all the juicy news she had.

"Actually, I can. What is it?"

"Well, I can't tell you if you're not listening to me, now can I?"

"If I wasn't listening to you, we wouldn't be having this conversation," he said, lowering the volume on the tv but his body still glued to it like a switched off Robocop.

"You are! If you were listening to me, you'd be paying attention to me, not the tv in front of you,"

"Amanda, do you need my eyes or ears to listen, because the last time I checked, I'm currently using them as they were intended, and this," turning to face his fiancé, "this helps nobody,"

"So what are you trying to tell me, watching tv is more important than paying attention to me?"

"When did I say that? Now you're putting words in my mouth and I've only said two sentences, none of which had the word important in them,"

"Well, your body language sure as hell implied it. You don't want to look or listen to me, You're angry and moody for no reason and don't want to speak or open up about what's wrong,"

"You know what's wrong?" Boitumelo paused the tv, facing Amanda. "You're what's wrong," he pointed.

"Me," she pointed in shock.

"Did I stutter? You want to talk about opening up and being honest, then what the hell is this?" Raising a wedding invite that was addressed to Sifiso. "I thought we'd had this discussion and I don't know why I have to repeat myself. I don't want your ex at my wedding."

"Why?"

"Why? What do you mean why? Amanda, there is no need for him to be there, finish and klaar. If the roles were reversed, we wouldn't be having this conversation in the first place. Secondly, we're both getting married, and as much as I want for you to have a memorable experience, I want the same for me. Having your ex cheer you on in the back row is not one of them,"

"But why?"

"What do you mean but why Amanda, I just told you why?"

"It doesn't make sense though, babe. It's not like he's going to be doing anything, and I don't know why you feel so threatened by him. We made a promise to one another long before we even knew we'd date each other back as friends that we'd attend one another's weddings and I'm just adhering to that deal," she shrugged.

"Well, I don't want him at my wedding end of discussion,"

"Then let that be his decision to decide because I'm not getting married without him there," Amanda said, folding her arms.

...

Pinky received an unexpected call from Boitumelo who spent most of his time making her giggle away before relaying the real reason for his call. It stunned her as much as it annoyed him, but all the cards were in place. Sifiso was home, after a bit of silence and listening to some ambient noise, he heard his deep voice fill the speakers in his car, which felt like the start of a news broadcast. Pinky felt like a commentator introducing two boxers at the beginning of the match as she explained who was on the other end, irrespective of this, his conversation was going to be swift. Once the small talk was over, there was only one thing that mattered.

"I'm calling because I just want to confirm seating arrangements for all the guests and I wanted to know whether you'd be attending?"

"No," Sifiso said quickly.

"Ok," Boitumelo said, dropping the call.

As soon as that fire died, a new one emerged as Pinky and Sfiso went toe to toe about why he was on loudspeaker in the first place. Pinky raised her palm to silence him.

"My phone, my rules,"

All her partner could do was fake a slap before running his hand through his head and swearing loudly and slamming the steering wheel in frustration.

"God, why me?" he whispered.

16

Sfiso began to regret his decision to come back home even though his intentions were pure. The constant barrage of questions that came from his mother about his life's decisions that led him to this point was beginning to get on his nerves and, unlike other people, he couldn't exactly tell his mother to fuck off. She found herself being transformed into a gospel track on replay on a Sunday morning when hearing the news about Amanda getting married. Sifiso sat opposite her on a couch, head crouched low as she continued to express her disappointment about how he could let her get away to the point where she got married. Although nothing was keeping him in the lounge, nothing to lock him within its four walls, it sure felt like a panic room. But he'd come this far, her disappointment in him no longer burned or was as effective as it started off and if anything would serve as a form of honest criticism as she had nothing to gain from lying to him.

His mother found out about his quandary of wanting to visit the person his beloved had previously loved, but not being able to do so out of honesty, faithfulness, and not wanting to be the cause of a broken marriage. The news came out with the assumption she'd side with him, see things from his perspective, not the "follow your heart crap," If he wanted to hear that there were plenty of people he could've headed to. Dr Woods, Brenda, the list was virtually endless. However, one thing Sfiso wasn't prepared for during his visit was the n's medical condition. Everyone was aware of the situation, but they'd learned to accept it, it was incredible that her health issues were getting worse considering that's what cancer did. Chemotherapy had done all it could and now it was faith to pick up where science had failed.

"So what happens now?" Sfiso asked. "Doctors aren't going to try anything new?"

"What do you mean what happens now, Sfiso? There's nothing else that can happen. You're how old now, 30? And I've had it for 33 of them, and in that time, each year I spent wondering if this was it, telling myself that this round of chemo was the one and there are only two things it taught me. The first is patience and the second- is"

"But Ma, you can't give up, look at how well things were going with chemo, yes, it wasn't the best, but you were living a long and healthy life. You can't just give up. Just like that,"

"And the second is acceptance." She finished. "I appreciate how you say it, as though we were both going through chemotherapy together. Listen Sfiso, I've accepted my place in life and what outcome it will be and for your sake, I pray that you find a way to do as well," she smiled.

"But Ma," Sfiso sulked.

"I love you,"

"I love you too, Ma," making his way over to his mother to embrace her tightly. "Does everybody else know?"

"Pretty much," she said after a while. "The problem was mostly breaking the news to you and a few others but for the most part, you," stroking the top of his head onto her chest.

"So how many months did the doctor say you have left?" he asked.

"Weh Sfiso, let's just focus and enjoy the present while we still can, Okay?"

"Okay,"

"So, are you going to the wedding?"

"Ma, let's just focus and enjoy the present while we still can, okay?" he said, raising his head from her chest.

"Touché,"

When Sfiso returned to Durban, he wasn't expecting to return to his role as a parent so quickly, picking up Lungelo from a mall, watching him angry or even worse, pissed off as fuck as he approached the car. His suspicions were correct as he slammed the door shut behind him and continued his sulking spree.

"Hey!"

"Sorry," Lungelo whispered

"What's wrong?"

"Nothing," Lungelo said, crossing his arms.

"Suit yourself then. I can't help you," his father replied, putting the car into gear and heading home.

"Love stinks," Lungelo said, clicking his tongue after a bout of silence filled with nothing but the radio.

"You can say that again," Sfiso sighed.

"If you wanted for us to break up, he should've just told me, not make a whole day out of it and make me spend money to be told that it's over. It's rubbish,"

"Ice cream?" Sifiso said.

The intention behind it was great and, in theory, perfect. But what was meant to be frozen milk and cream ended up being Lungelo's first beer and his father's... a number he'd stopped counting a long time ago ended up putting his son in a much better mood. A mood so good it would have Pinky pull Sifiso to the side as they entered the house and quietly sat him down on the bed.

"I've been thinking and I've given this a lot of thought,"

"Ya," he said, raising an eyebrow.

"I want us, I want you to go to that wedding. Despite all the issues that have come up and what's been said so far,"

"Why?"

"I think it's what's best,"

"For who?" he said, jumping to his feet.

"Like I stated, it resulted in a lot of issues between us that could've been avoided and brought a few to the surface that I hadn't even considered. We'll always have problems and the best way to solve them is to face them head-on, and unfortunately for my case, talking about this is part of tackling a problem head-on," Pinky sighed.

"And what happens if it's something I don't want to do anymore, for no other reason other than being happy with not going?"

"Then I guess we'll have to cancel the flight and accommodation,"

"What? Why do you even have it in the first place when you heard him loud and clear ask if I wanted to come and I told him in front of both of you that I didn't? What don't the both of you understand, or is there something going on that neither of you want to tell me?"

"No, nothing like that," she said after some time.

"And that's perfectly fine. That silence said more than I needed to hear, thank you," standing up. "And I hope, for your sake, whatever the two of you got planned works out." Before giving his son a fist bump and leaving.

17

B renda sipped on her drink and listened to Amanda's explanation of what happened for what must've been the umpteenth time. She was silent, no dramatic interruptions to spur her on, attentive and gave her, her full attention with just simple movements of body language and eye contact. It was something which could've been avoided had Mr Molefe learnt to do the same. However, his inability to do so provided nothing more than a retreating tide just before a tsunami, revealing a lot of things left ashore, meant to be underwater. Amanda's inability to get married without the presence of Sfiso, keeping a childhood promise or not, the fact of the matter was they'd broken up and if she was really over him like she claimed she was, then she'd get married without him. Better still, she should be grateful for having a partner that was only found in romance novels, one that had already let it go and was ready to forgive despite all the chaos it caused before their special day. The letter, the proclamation for his undying love, Boity, and how she'd act if the roles were reversed. Throwing a tantrum and risking it all for an ex was not worth it.

"Are you even listening to me?"

"Yes, Amanda, how can I not, you sound like a self-help video. Question is, are you listening to me?"

Amanda fell silent.

"Thank you. Now, don't mind me and my silence. I'm just trying to piece together the missing pieces," Brenda took a sip out of her cup. "There are a few things I don't understand, that's all,"

"Oh,"

"So, are you seriously going to let all this money and preparation go to waste? You're not going to get married unless your ex doesn't pitch?"

"Well then, if you put it like that, you make it seem bad but-" Amanda stuttered.

"What other way is there to put it?" drinking out her cup, "Am I lying?" Brenda asked.

"No, but-"

"But what, you have everything in front of you and more, my only question to you is why do you want to keep going back? In fact, there are plenty, but for the sake of time, I'll ask one. I've known both of you and annoyingly been around long enough to know that it can only be one thing. Question is... in your little box of secrets does he know?"

"Who?"

"That's the million-dollar question, isn't it?" Brenda asked.

"Brenda, listen. I need him here, he needs to know about-"

"Need or want, because there's a big difference between the two. If he needs to know so urgently, send him a message or call him. If you don't think you can do that, then send me like you've been doing this whole while, if I can do the same thing an email can be much faster. You see, I see no reason why I can't tell him if you're too lazy to do the aforementioned solutions. Besides, you're marrying a doctor for God's sake, if he can't help you, he can get you someone who can. If that doesn't make sense, then I shouldn't be here either,"

"They're back," Amanda sighed.

"Who?" Brenda asked, confused.

"The Polyps,"

"Well, that explains a lot now, doesn't it," she said, finishing her drink. "But Boity is a surgeon, can't he cut them out?"

"He's not that type of surgeon. Look, I just want him here, or at least see him before I tie the knot and live my happily ever after and explain to him why things ended up the way that they did. I think I'm ready," touching her chest, "and now I think he's ready to hear it too before it's too late,"

18

From Amanda to Sfiso, Brenda was a role as she set about finding out what the problem was with her friend. The last thing she wanted was to come in between them and be forced to choose because it wouldn't be a happy ending for either of them. With Sfiso it was easy, he didn't want to come; it was simple as that, but she was able to make him go, not because Amanda wanted him there but because she wanted him there. It just so happened that the venue involved Amanda and her new man. That was the problem with Sfiso, if you knew what to say to him, you could play him like a piano, but for the sake of urgency, using him as a keyboard was what would work best. Rather than playing the having them as a trio at her wedding card, she'd picked a side, and it was his side. She simply didn't want to go to that wedding alone because unlike him, she didn't have bad blood with anybody and so her attendance was paramount. But at the same time on a personal level she didn't want to go alone. Her friend feeling sad for her friend decided to accompany Brenda despite what it entailed and for some reason it made all parties happy, Pinky included. With Sfiso, it made sense, but there they were in Jo'burg, getting ready to attend the function of the year. Sfiso's appearance to Amanda was a surprise. Her happiness aside, he was also human and had feelings and so those had also played a part despite being a date for Brenda.

•••

Amanda was at a loss for words when she saw Sfiso with her own eyes, but when she heard Brenda telling her to stop bitching and acting like a spoilt bitch, it finally made sense. Her dream wedding could continue and it would do so thanks to a little help from Brenda. Sfiso spent all of his free time trying to blend into the background with a somewhat level of success, not the best, but it was good enough for him to see how happy Amanda was around the doctor. Although it made him jealous, he promised himself to keep his cool and not cause a scene in a public place or cause a scene, period. But the more he watched as a bystander and not as a partner getting shunned to the side the more he began to see what he assumed were his and his ex-girlfriend's partner's true colours as they lapped up each other's attention as though they were on a first date thanks to a matchmaking app and not a gate crasher to one another's wedding.

It was at the after-party where people finally realised his presence, first the lady of the hour when she was out greeting all the guests for attending her special day to which he kept things cordial and brief. The next was to her friend Brenda. By the time Brenda tried to intervene and ensure Sifiso remained a proper date it was already too late. Sfiso had traversed down a long road when it came to fermented fruit, and the signs of returning seemed slim. Slurring most of his words and refusing glasses of water just as many times he found it hard to grab the glasses in front of his line of sight. The two had always joked how loud drunks who were often the life of the party were the best drunks to have around because they wore out the fastest like a person ignoring the fuel light in a sports car. The quiet drunks on the other hand, those people were dangerous because you didn't know for how long they'd been feeling like that as well as how much more alcohol they could handle because they never showed it. But it was safe to assume by the two quarts of empty beer bottles and an array of shots that lay across the table Sfiso was wasted. Even more than usual due to the mix of alcohol, a complete no-no.

"Alright buddy, I think you've had enough," she said, trying to lift her friend off the chair only to drop him on the floor. "Oops,"

Sfiso lay motionless on the floor, almost immune to what had just happened to him, either that or in need to absorb the pain before any movement. Either way, his motionless state made his friend feel uncomfortable and guilty even more so since she was the entire reason he was on the floor in the first place. But he put her fears to rest when his coughs turned out to be failed attempts at preventing himself from crying.

"Ah bullshit, I didn't drop you that hard. Enough with the dramatics," Brenda sighed, before giving it another try.

"She's gone," he whimpered into her ear.

"I know buddy, and that's okay. We'll find someone new, I promise,"

"She's gone," throwing himself into Brenda and digging his face into her for a place to cry properly. "My mother's gone and I couldn't be there at the very last moment to say goodbye cause I'm stuck attending this piece of shit,"

"I'm so sorry," Brenda managed to whisper, clutching her bestie tightly. Although she didn't yet know the pain of losing a parent, the emotional state Sfiso was currently in took more of an emotional turmoil on her than him. She'd never seen him like this and therefore genuinely didn't know how to act, what to say without it feeling disingenuous or as though they were words used to do nothing more than shut him up.

"Bitch, get off my man!" Amanda shouted from across the room, unlocking herself from her embrace from Boitumelo as they slow danced.

"Everything okay here?" Boitumelo asked, hot on Amanda's heels, along with all the attention she'd managed to garner.

"Yes," Brenda stuttered. "He's just had too much to drink that's all,"

"Oh my God, Sfiso, are you okay? What happened?" she asked, shoving her way past onlookers and kneeling beside him as though she were about to change a flat tyre.

"Amanda, no," Brenda told her, pushing her away and looking up at her husband. One she either hadn't noticed was staring down at her disapprovingly or choosing to ignore him on purpose.

"She's gone," Sfiso cried.

"I'm right here, I'm not going anywhere," she reassured him, rubbing his back.

"Amanda," Brenda sighed, moving Sfiso away from her.

"What's going on, why won't you let me help him? He's my friend as well," she told her.

"I think he's a little more than that I've seen enough," Boitumelo interrupted.

Amanda turned around in shock, irritated at the fact that she was caught off guard more than anything else. But this wasn't the time to start arguing, again, over minuscule and nonsensical things, it was her wedding day for crying out loud. That's right, her wedding day and yet she was knelt down beside her ex, by his side when he needed someone that loved him most, not with the perfect man.

Silence.

19

She stood up, adjusting the invisible creases that were on her dress as she found the ideal height to stare her husband in the eye and ignore those that had gathered around her. If eyes could speak then there's nothing that Boitumelo needed more to say with those that were red and glazed. The man didn't cry and there were countless others to vouch for him but even if he had nobody would've blamed him given what he'd seen. But it wasn't so much what he'd seen but how he'd seen it, after all, there was nothing wrong with comforting a person who'd lost a parent. However, the problem lay with the fight your own wife put up at all odds to be the one they cried their grieving shoulder against. Proof, that the blame lay not with Sfiso, a man who didn't want to be there in the first place, whose attention was more fixated on a woman he'd never see again and regretting passing up the last chance to do so, but with Amanda. A woman who vowed not to get married to him unless the same man she now comforted like a teddy bear to a toddler wasn't there, realising all of his fears before him without any intention on his behalf. "What now?" he thought to himself. He'd tied the knot, second thoughts were no longer an option.

He turned around and left his wife. Figuratively, emotionally and physically as he disappointed everybody around him in anticipation of a confrontation. As a medical professional, he'd been in the industry long enough to be groomed when to switch off his emotions and think with his head and not his heart, even if it felt hard doing the former. If there was any consolation, he would manage to go console the one individual who had given him attention in the entirety of his pre and post-days of marriage, Pinky.

Finding her, however, was a different story, but worth it. Finding her in a bar like they'd agreed, playing with the straw in her drink, he snuck up behind her and gave her a fright. One that would be the first of many as he rocked her world, forcing her to call out deities while she, in return, made him scrunch his toes like he had a medical condition.

Amanda tried turning her attention back towards Sfiso but was shunned away by Brenda, who forced her to go look for and patch things with her man since she was a married woman and had no business being around Sfiso and her in the first place. Checking up on them was admirable in the first place, but she had to face facts, if she chose Boitumelo then she would have to leave Sfiso behind irrespective of what happened in his life and his being at this wedding was an exception. It was a hard pill to swallow but Brenda was right, unfortunately so, and just like the veil behind her forehead at the end of a wedding speech, they were behind her as she set off in search of Boitumelo to apologise and make amends. When she did find Boitumelo, she wasn't prepared for what she saw, nor would she in her wildest dreams. The man truly lived by an out-of-sight, out-of-mind philosophy to the core. He sat alongside Sfiso's partner, getting cosy as they shared drinks, laughed and ignored her as they enjoyed themselves at the bar provided with their hotel room, half naked and gathering energy for the next round of supposed activities of adultery.

"Babe, can we talk," she cleared her throat.

"Sure," wiping a stray tear from the hard amount of laughing he was doing.

"Alone," emphasising the word.

"No, no, no. It doesn't work like that, sweetie. Besides, anything you want to say to me you can say in front of her, if it's not related to her man then chances are she'll have long forgotten about it by the time she heads home," Boitumelo said, waving a stray finger at her wife.

Amanda sighed deeply and watched his husband resume the chitter-chatter, ignoring her as if she didn't exist. The trip towards the bar needed her to be honest with herself and honest with all parties, money was a beautiful veil that worked for most people but it came at a cost. It dug you out and left you as nothing but a shell of your former self. "I can't do this anymore,"

"Well, good for you. Now you know how I felt this entire wedding with you pining over your ex-lover, maybe now you've learnt to consider other people's feelings," he finished, turning to face her. "I'm glad you realised that not everything is about you a-"

"I'm sorry," she said, handing him her ring and wiping her face.

"What are you doing?" he asked, glancing at the ring in confusion. "Amanda!!" he shouted, watching her walk away.

A hand from behind grabbed the ring from behind and swivelled him in his chair. Pinky raised his sunken face and looked him in the eye as she placed the ring on the bar table beside them.

"Experience trumps talent, remember that," placing her hand on his cheek and smiling at him. He gingerly returned the gesture before she spun him around and poured him a drink. "To heartbreak,"

"To heartbreak," they toasted.

fin

Don't miss out!

Visit the website below and you can sign up to receive emails whenever Londa Cele publishes a new book. There's no charge and no obligation.

https://books2read.com/r/B-A-XGKG-KZKGC

BOOKS 2 READ

Connecting independent readers to independent writers.